Sunny's Royal Ball

Adapted by Courtney Carbone

Based on the teleplay "The Royal Visit"
by Brian Hohlfeld

Illustrated by Francesco Legramandi and Giulia Priori

A GOLDEN BOOK • NEW YORK

T#: 551963
ISBN 978-1-5247-6855-3
rhcbooks.com
Printed in the United States of America
10 9 8 7 6 5 4 3 2 1

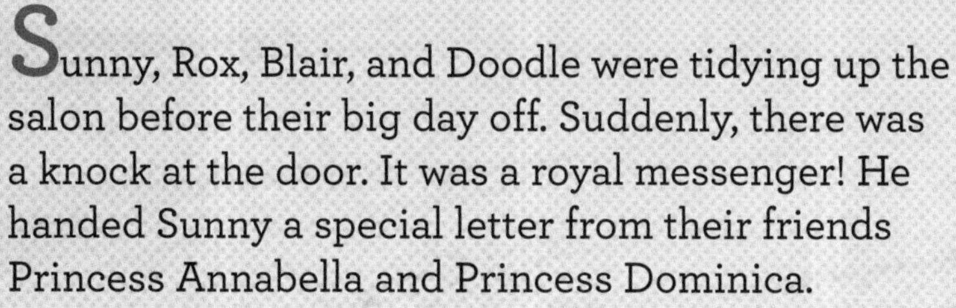

Sunny, Rox, Blair, and Doodle were tidying up the salon before their big day off. Suddenly, there was a knock at the door. It was a royal messenger! He handed Sunny a special letter from their friends Princess Annabella and Princess Dominica.

"It's an invitation to the palace!" Sunny exclaimed. They were going to have a royal day.

The friends zoomed to the castle in the Glam Van. When they arrived, the princesses greeted them with hugs.

"You made it!" Princess Annabella said. "Welcome to our home!"

"This place is amazing!" exclaimed Blair.

"It's so good to see you all!" Princess Dominica said.

"We're hosting a ball tonight!" Princess Annabella told them.

Rox couldn't believe her ears. "A royal ball? With royal music and royal food and royal . . . stuff?"

"I'm so excited!" squealed Blair. "But I didn't bring anything to dance in."

Princess Annabella took them upstairs to her royal closet. There were rows of beautiful gowns and matching shoes!

"You can wear whatever you want," she offered.

The girls picked out their outfits. Doodle even got a fancy bow tie for his collar!

“Now we need princess hairstyles to match!” said Sunny. “It’s Glam Van time!”

Soon everyone’s hair looked elegant.

“Perfect!” Princess Dominica told them.

“We’re having a ceremony to honor our cousin Prince Dudley,” said Princess Annabella. “And we’d like you to take part in it!”

Just then, a soccer ball came flying through an open door of the Glam Van! Rox blocked it from hitting anyone.

The ball belonged to Prince Dudley, who jumped into the van to retrieve it.

"Out of my way!" he shouted.

Sunny's friend Timmy ran up to the van and peered in. He was Prince Dudley's driver for the day.

Sunny went to get the ball. "Let me help you with that," she said.

"A prince does *not* need help!" Prince Dudley replied gruffly.

Later, when it was time to rehearse for the royal ceremony, Prince Dudley struggled to learn the steps in the ceremonial march.

"I can help," Sunny told him brightly. "You can walk with me and do what I do."

"I don't need your help!" yelled the prince. "Besides, I have better things to do, like explore the woods with Timmy." He stormed off, and Timmy followed.

Later, Sunny got a frantic call from Timmy.
"Prince Dudley and I found an old tower," he said, "and now we're locked inside it! Can you help us?"
They could hear the prince's voice in the background. "I don't need any help!" he said.
"Don't worry!" said Sunny. "We're on our way!"

Sunny and her friends drove into the woods and found the tower. They spotted Timmy and Prince Dudley in the upstairs window.

"What are you doing here?" the prince demanded. "I told you—I can handle this!"

Rox and Blair pulled on the tower door as hard as they could, but it was no use. The door was locked! Sunny tried to pick the lock with her comb, but it didn't work.

“This is just like my favorite fairy tale,” said Blair, “where the prince climbs up the tower using Rapunzel’s hair.”

“Only this time, it’s the *prince* in the tower,” said Rox. “And his hair isn’t very long.”

That gave Sunny an idea.

“The prince may not have long hair, but *we* do!” she said.

Sunny got some hair extensions from the van. Then she and her friends wove them together to create a rope.

“I don’t need your help!” insisted Prince Dudley.

“I know, Your Highness,” Sunny replied. “But Timmy does!”

Sunny made a slingshot out of some hair bands, then shot the rope toward the open window. She climbed the rope all the way up!

Timmy was happy to see Sunny—but Prince Dudley still didn't want her help.

Sunny and Timmy raced downstairs, and Sunny used her comb to unlock the door from the inside. It worked!

Now they had to get to the royal ceremony! Prince Dudley refused to come down, so everyone pretended to leave without him.

Suddenly, Prince Dudley ran after them.

"Wait!" he called. He didn't want to be alone in the woods. "I'm sorry. I guess I do need help . . . with a lot. I just don't like to admit that I can't do some things by myself."

"Everybody needs help sometimes," said Sunny.

They made it back to the castle just in time for the royal ball!

"Would you mind walking with me?" the prince asked Sunny. "I could use the help. I want to make sure I get it right."

Together they marched down the aisle, using the special steps she had helped him learn.

"Welcome, Prince Dudley!" Princess Dominica announced.

The royal subjects cheered loudly.

"Thank you, everyone, for all your help," Prince Dudley said, addressing the crowd. He smiled warmly at Sunny, who smiled back. "Now let's start the party!"

The royal ball began, and everyone danced. Doodle showed off his favorite moves. They were all having so much fun, they didn't want the magical night to end!

Luckily, there were still some surprises in store for Sunny and her friends.

"Keep the dresses," Princess Annabella said. "Our gift to you!"

"And why don't you stay after the ball?" Princess Dominica said. "We can have a sleepover!"

They all agreed that it had been a perfect day off—and a royal sleepover was a great way to finish the night!